The Boy Who Cried Wolf

An Aesop fable retold by
Elizabeth Adams and Daniel Howarth

W

Once upon a time, there was a shepherd boy who looked after a flock of sheep. Every day, he left his village and took his sheep up into the hills nearby.

At first, the shepherd boy loved his job. But soon he got bored of doing the same thing every day. The sheep were no fun. They just ate grass all day long.

"If only something would happen!" he thought to himself.

The shepherd boy's job was important. There were wolves roaming in the hills. If he spotted a wolf, he had to warn the villagers.

One day, when he was bored, the shepherd boy decided to play a trick.
"Wolf! Wolf!" he cried.

The villagers stopped what they were doing. They ran as fast as they could up to the hills to help the shepherd boy.

When the villagers arrived, they were out of breath. The shepherd boy couldn't stop giggling. "I tricked you all!" he laughed. "There isn't a wolf at all!"

The villagers were annoyed.

"Don't do that again!" they told

the shepherd boy.

A few weeks later, the shepherd boy was bored again. "It was so funny when they all ran up," he thought. He knew that he would be in trouble, but …

… he just couldn't help himself.

"The look on their faces will

be even funnier this time!"

he thought.

"Wolf! Wolf!" he cried,

as loudly as he could.

15

Again the villagers stopped what they were doing. Again they ran as fast as they could up to the hills to help the shepherd boy.

When the villagers arrived, the shepherd boy was rolling on the floor laughing. "Tricked you again!" he panted between snorts.

The villagers were really cross this time. "We told you not to do that again!" they shouted at the shepherd boy. "Next time you cry wolf, we won't be so quick to come and help you!"

The very next day, a wolf really did come. "Wolf! Wolf!" cried the shepherd boy at the top of his voice.

"WOLF! WOLF!"

The boy shouted and shouted.
The sheep were being chased
far away by the wolf.

"Why aren't they coming?
Can't they hear me?"
thought the shepherd boy.

The villagers could hear the shepherd boy, but they didn't want to be tricked again. So they just ignored him.

26

"I'm not running up that hill just to make him laugh," they said to each other.

The boy tried his best, but he couldn't find his sheep. That evening, he had to come back without them. The shepherd boy felt very ashamed.

About the story

The Boy who Cried Wolf is a fable by Aesop. Aesop was a slave and a storyteller who is believed to have lived in ancient Greece between 620 and 560 BCE, making this story over 2,500 years old. A fable is a story that contains a lesson. This story shows that if you are a liar, you might not be believed even when you are telling the truth.

Be in the story!

Imagine you are
the shepherd boy.
You have to explain
what has happened
to the sheep.

Now imagine you are
the villagers. What
would you say to
the shepherd boy?
How can you make
him stop telling lies?

First published in 2014 by
Franklin Watts
338 Euston Road
London
NW1 3BH

Franklin Watts Australia
Level 17/207 Kent Street
Sydney
NSW 2000

A CIP catalogue record for this book is available
from the British Library.

The artwork for this story first appeared in
Leapfrog: The Boy Who Cried Wolf

ISBN 978 1 4451 2831 3 (hbk)
ISBN 978 1 4451 2832 0 (pbk)
ISBN 978 1 4451 2834 4 (library ebook)
ISBN 978 1 4451 2833 7 (ebook)

Series Editor: Jackie Hamley
Series Advisor: Catherine Glavina
Series Designer: Cathryn Gilbert

Printed in China

Franklin Watts is a divison of
Hachette Children's Books,
an Hachette UK company.
www.hachette.co.uk